mOm,
Mac&Cheese,
PLEASE!

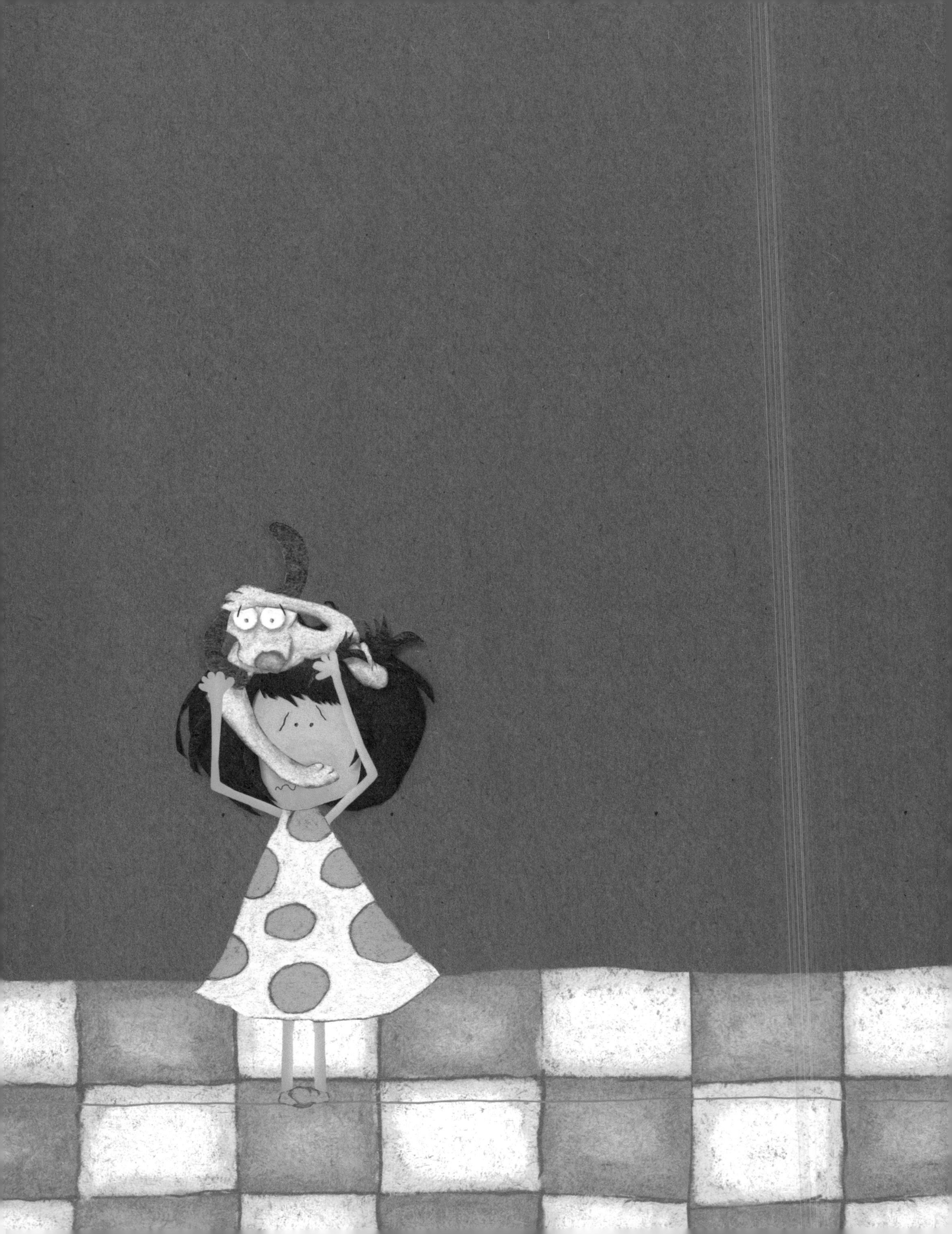

mOm, Mac&Cheese, PLEASE!

Written by Marilyn Olin
Illustrated by Dunja Pantic

Sky Pony Press
New York

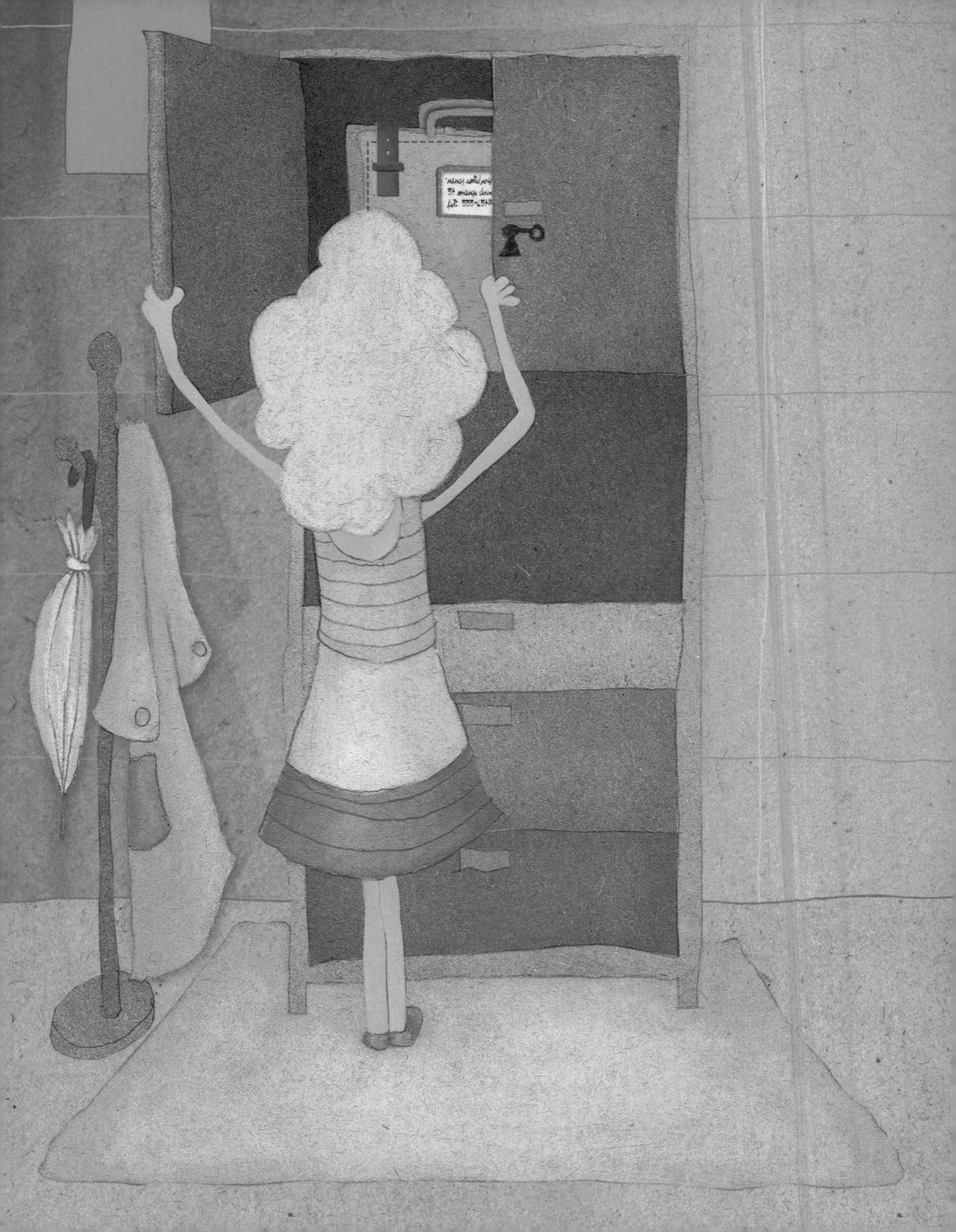
57 orange
tel. 555-

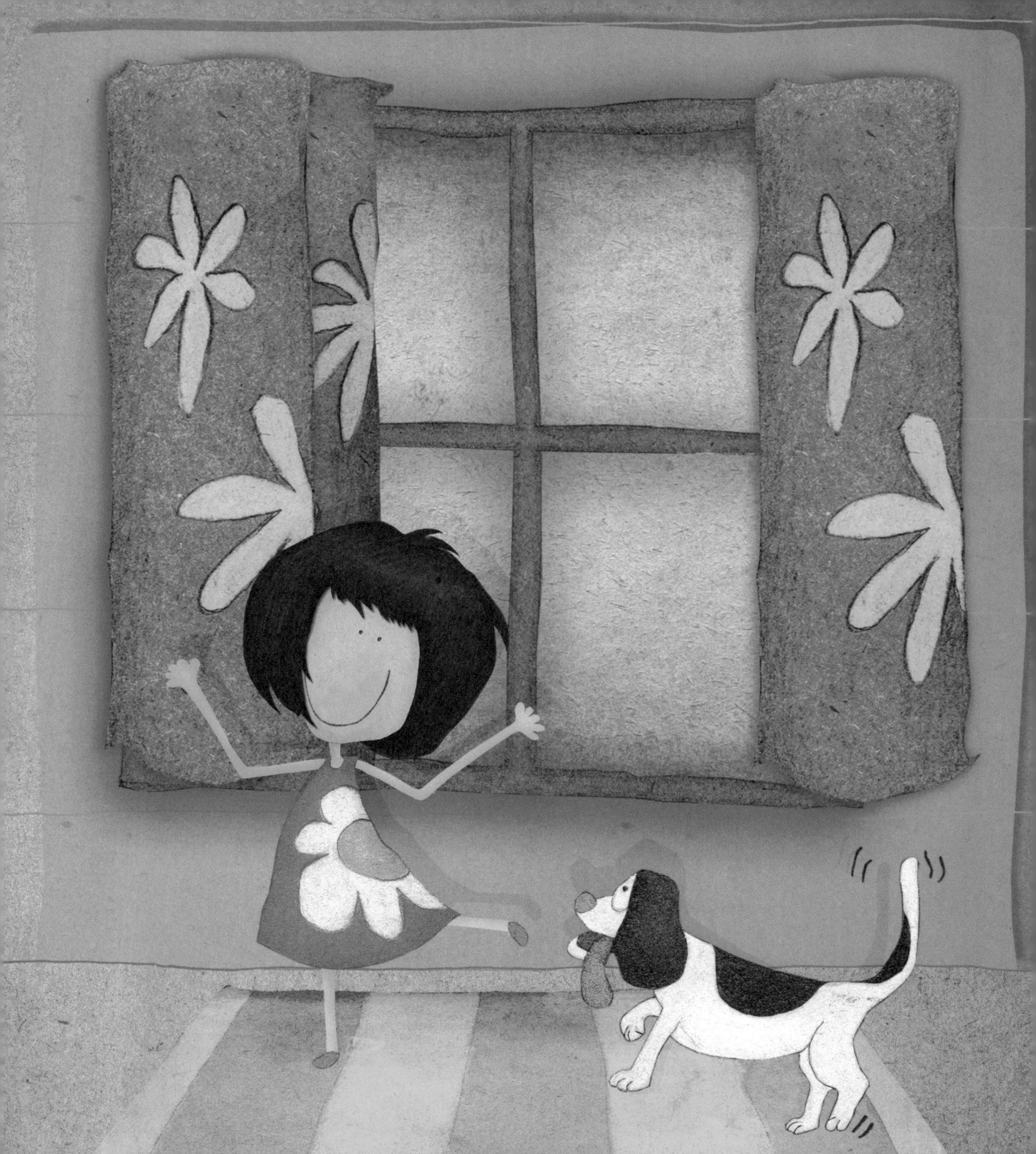

My mother stopped working. I thought it was cool . . .

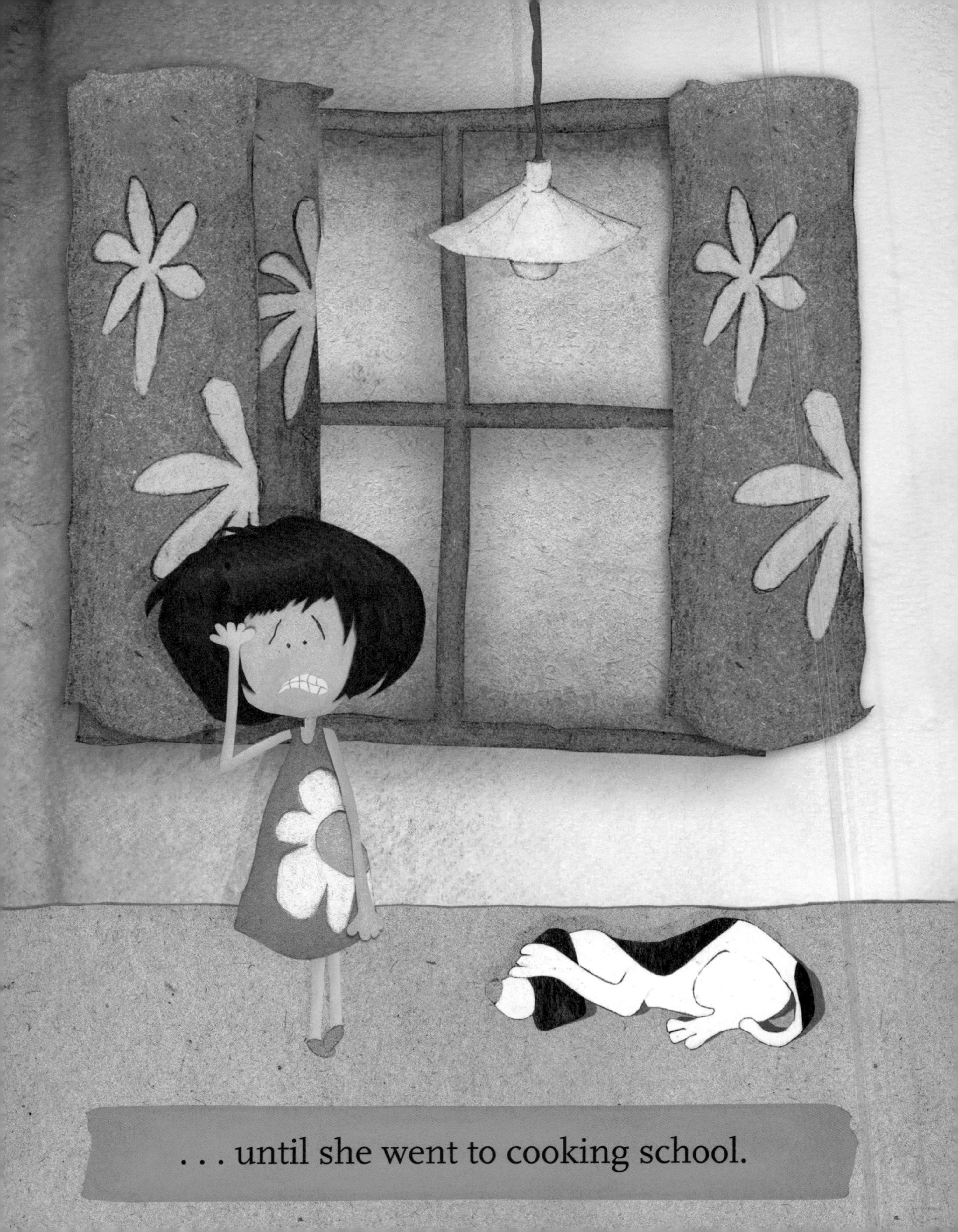

. . . until she went to cooking school.

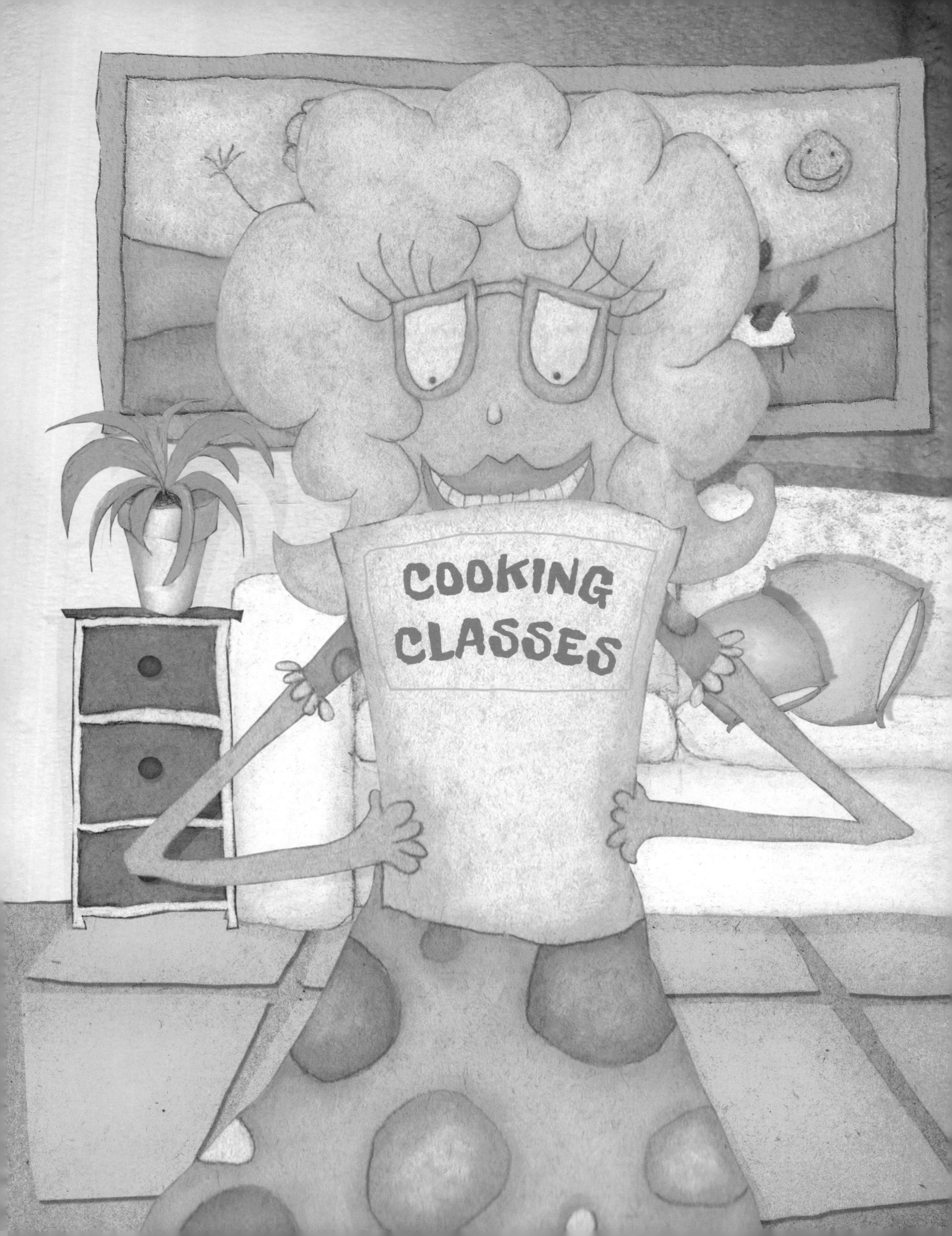
COOKING
CLASSES

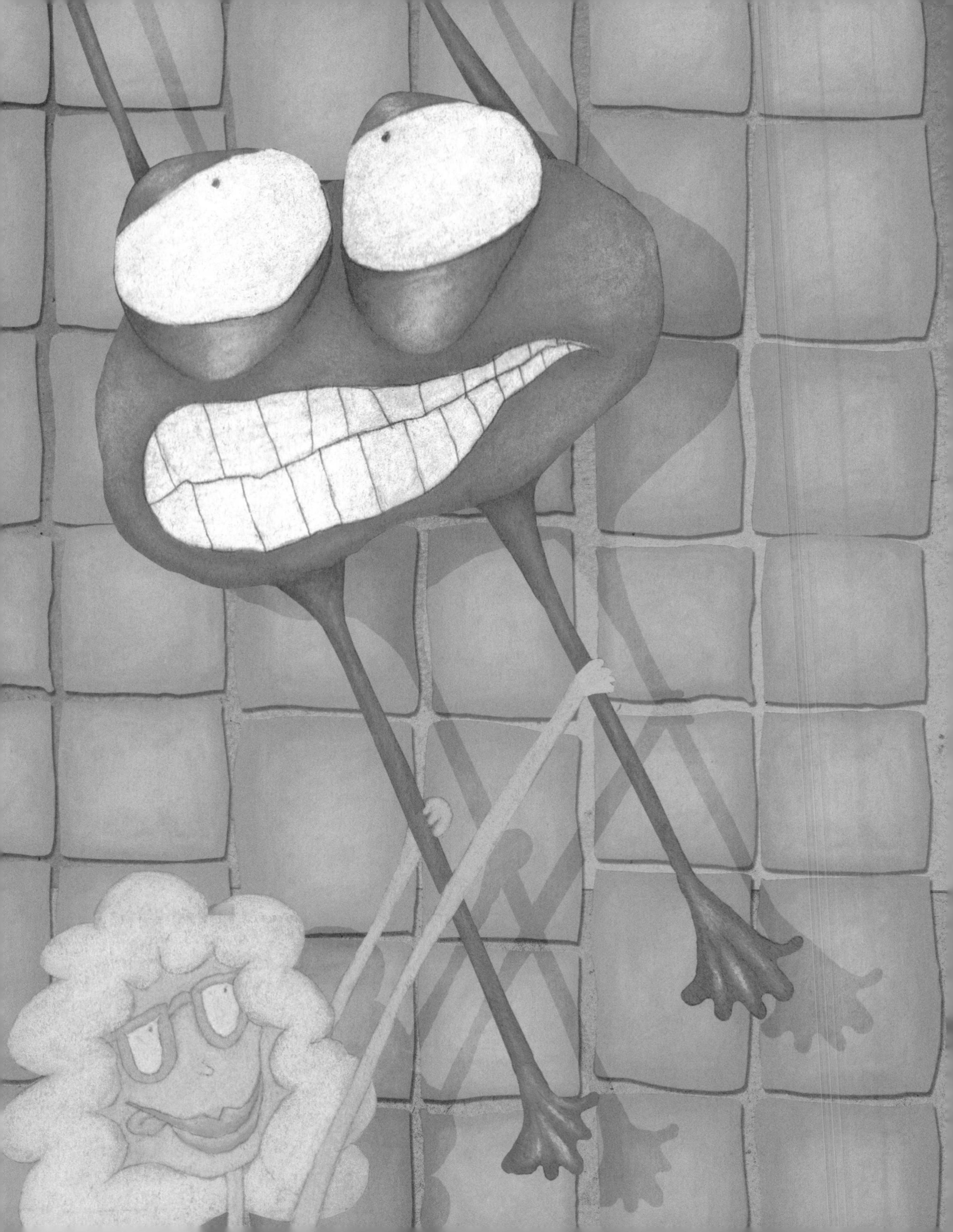

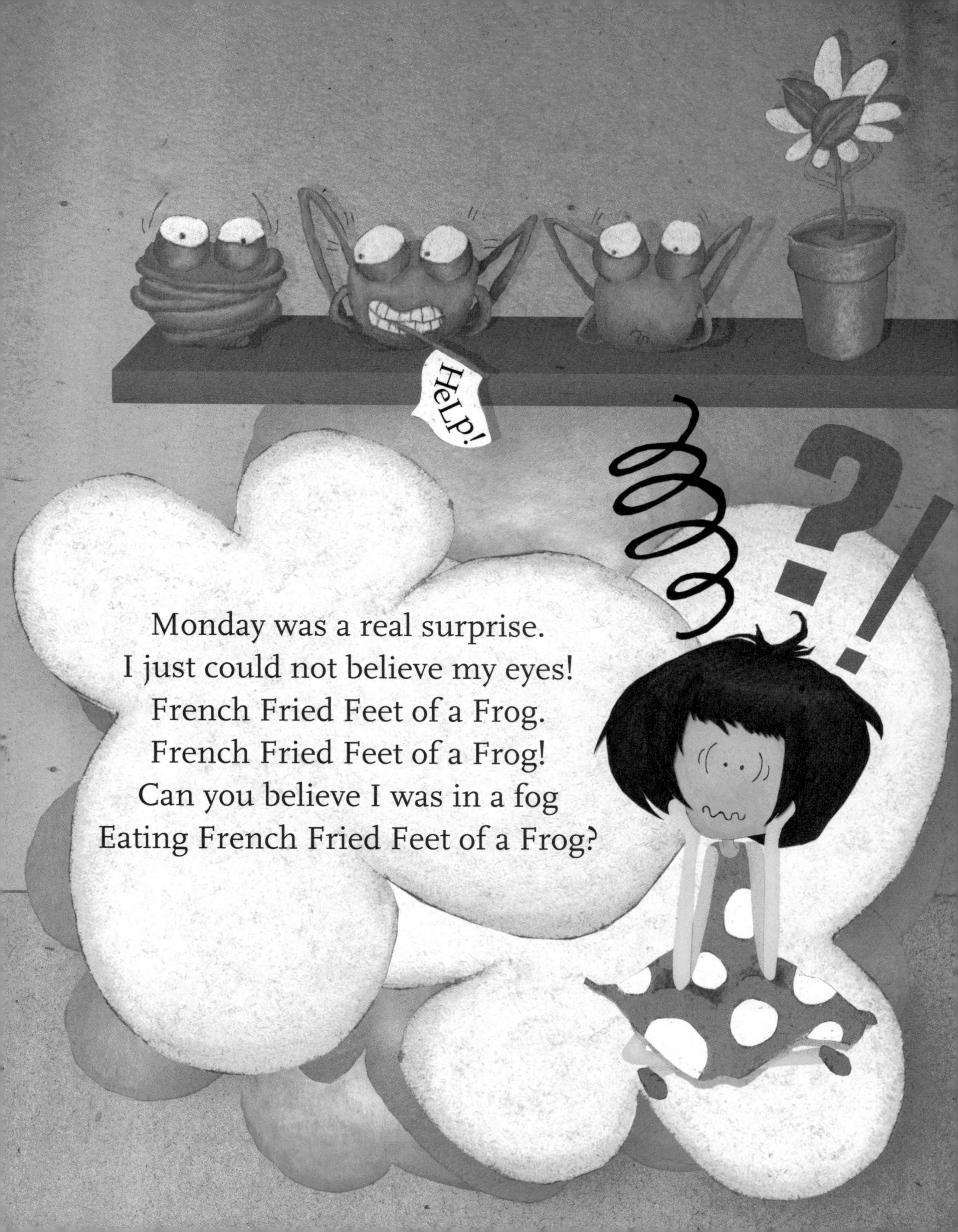
HeLp!

Monday was a real surprise.
I just could not believe my eyes!
French Fried Feet of a Frog.
French Fried Feet of a Frog!
Can you believe I was in a fog
Eating French Fried Feet of a Frog?

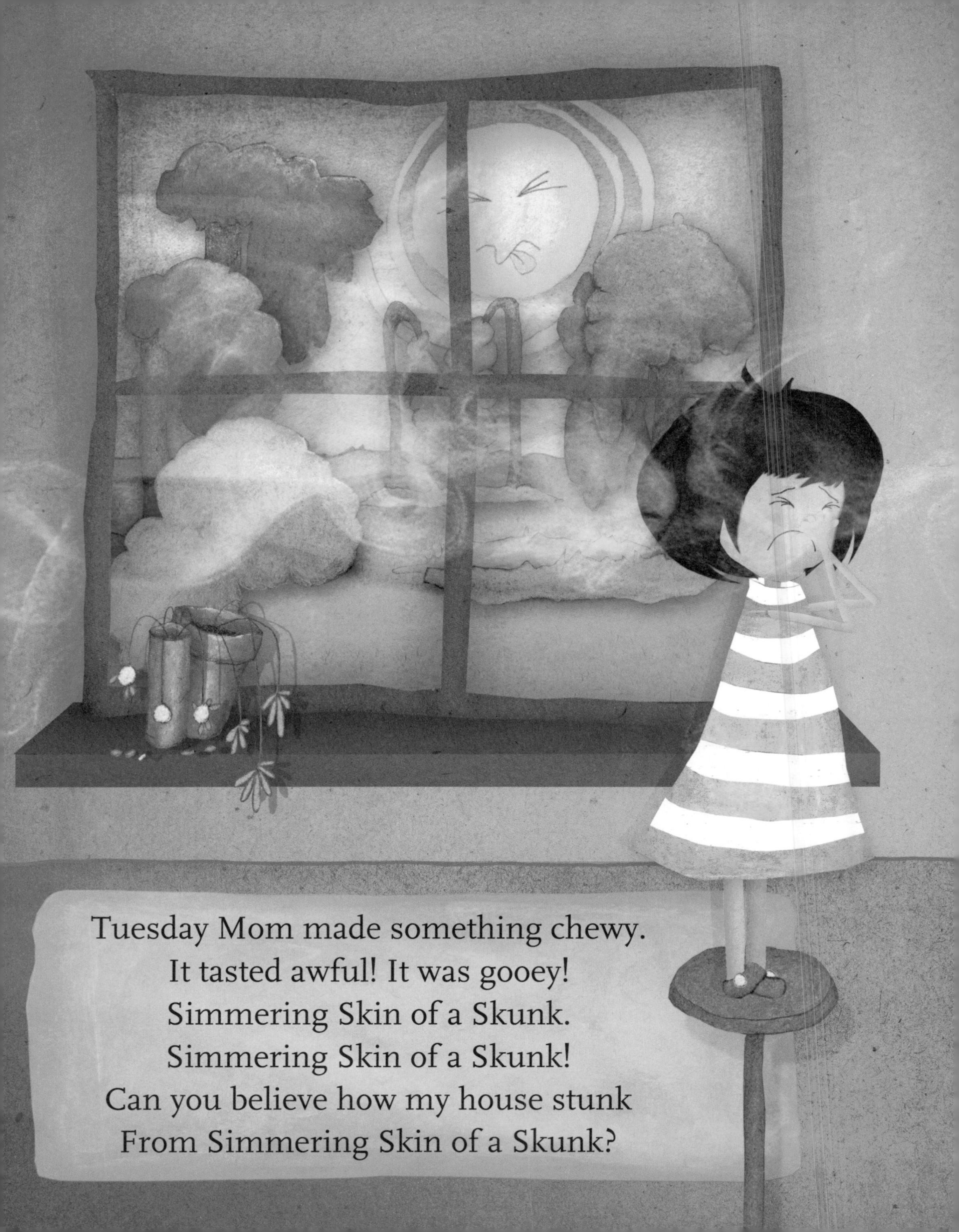

Tuesday Mom made something chewy.
It tasted awful! It was gooey!
Simmering Skin of a Skunk.
Simmering Skin of a Skunk!
Can you believe how my house stunk
From Simmering Skin of a Skunk?

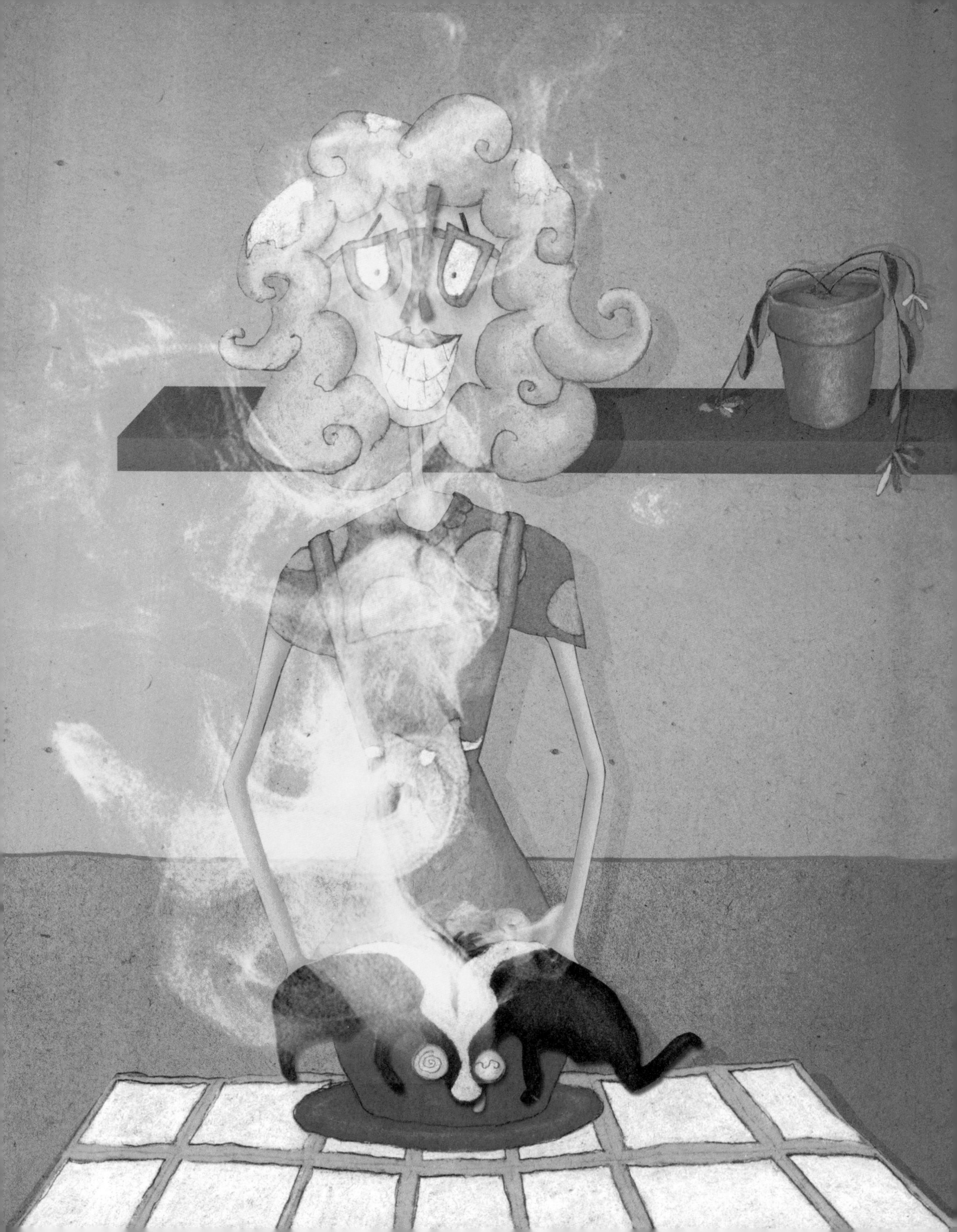

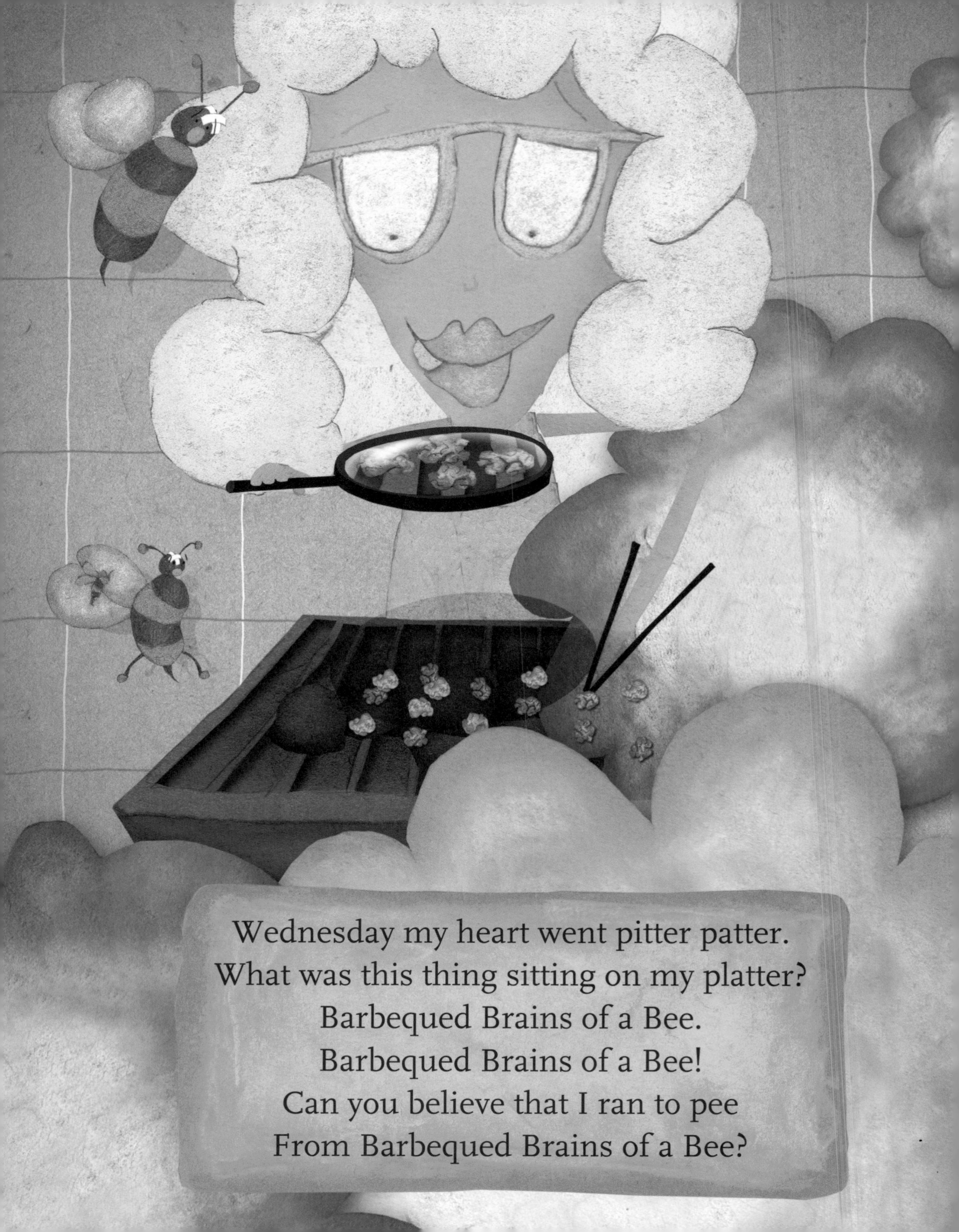

Wednesday my heart went pitter patter.
What was this thing sitting on my platter?
Barbequed Brains of a Bee.
Barbequed Brains of a Bee!
Can you believe that I ran to pee
From Barbequed Brains of a Bee?

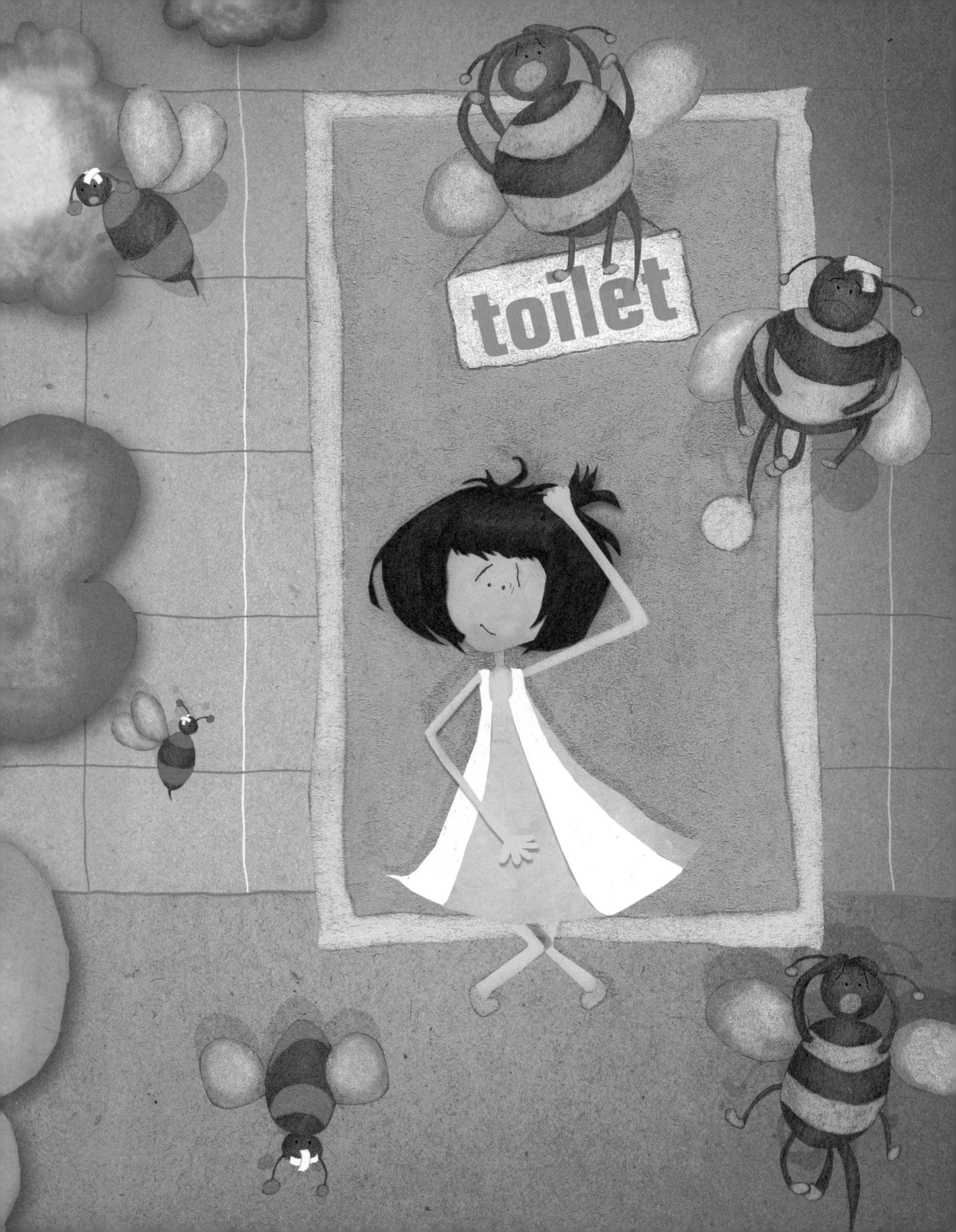
toilet

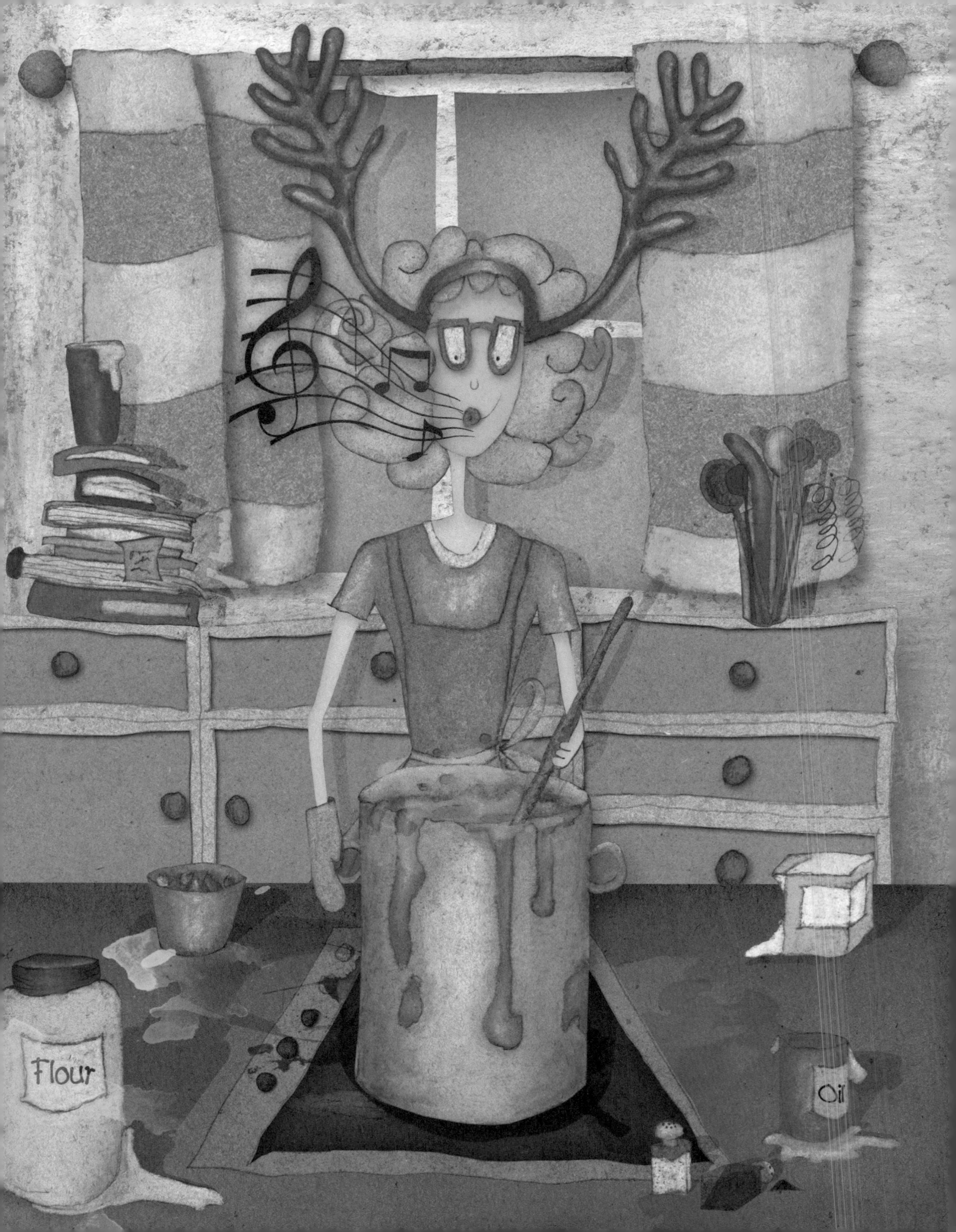
Flour
Oil

Thursday something weird was brewing.
Whatever could my mom be doing?
Marmalade Mouth of a Moose.
Marmalade Mouth of a Moose!
Can you believe my tooth came loose
Eating Marmalade Mouth of a Moose?

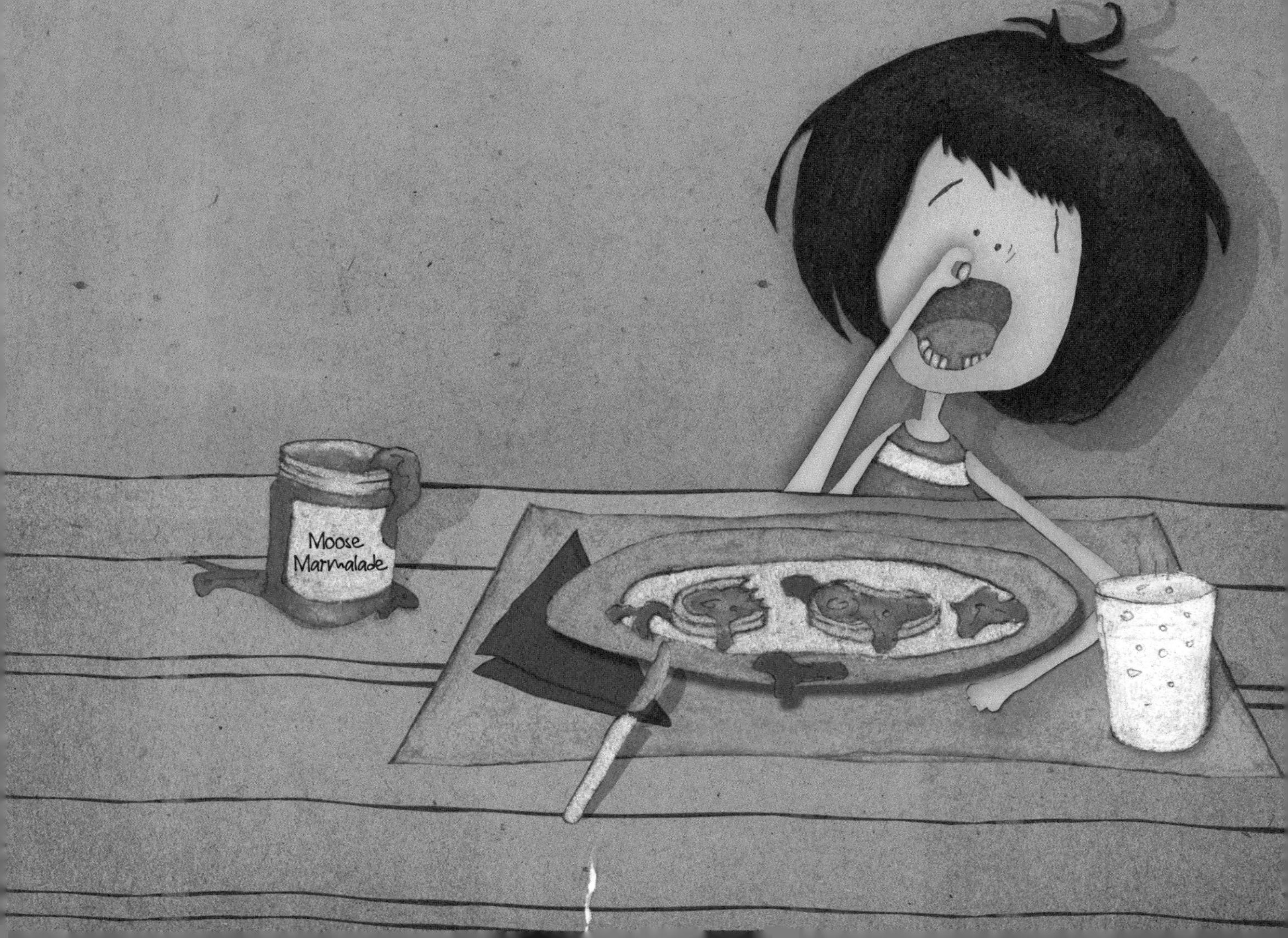
Moose Marmalade

On Friday my whole house was shaking.
What on earth was my mom baking?
Caramelized Croc in a cup.
Caramelized Croc in a cup!
Can you believe that I threw up
Eating Caramelized Croc in a cup?

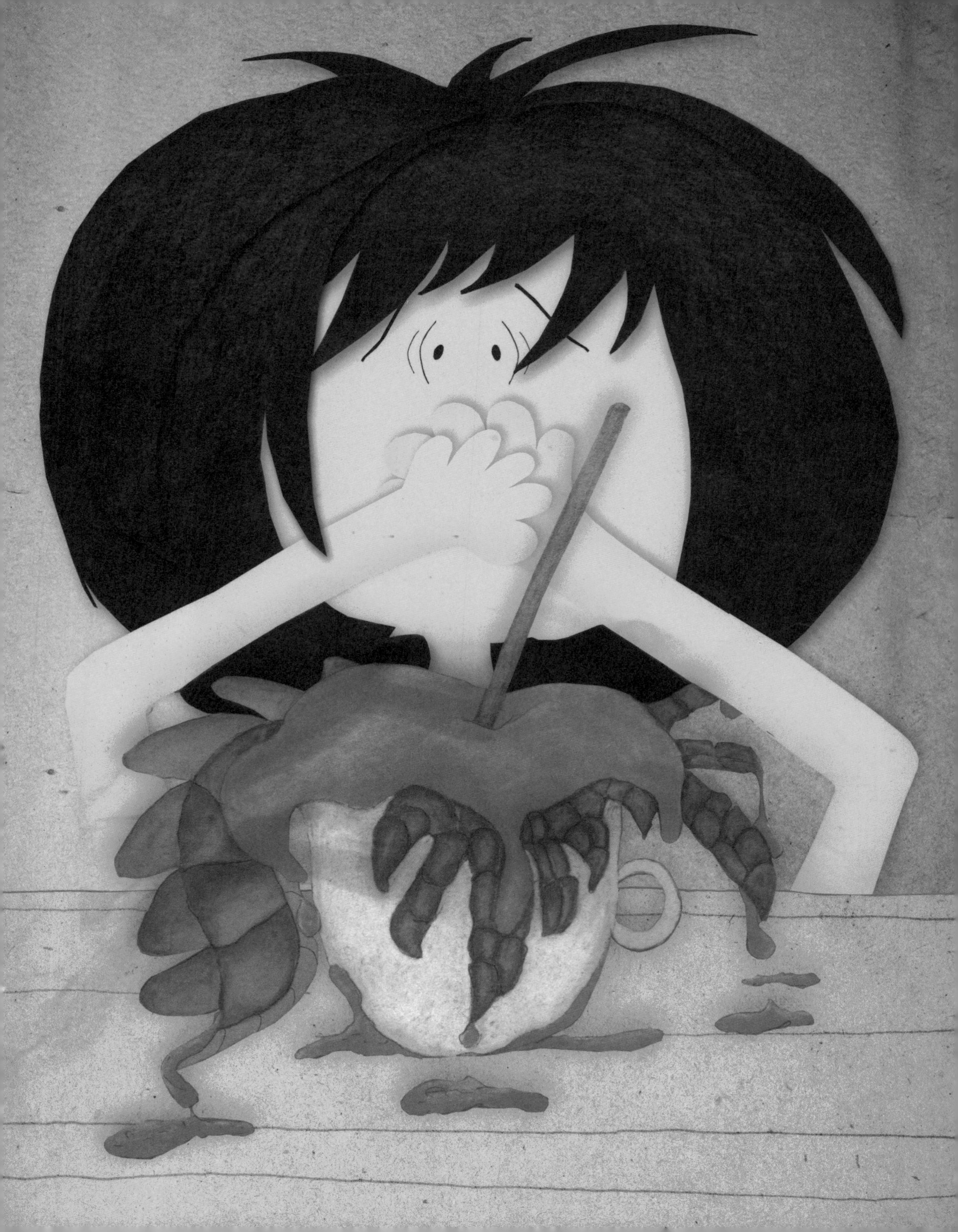

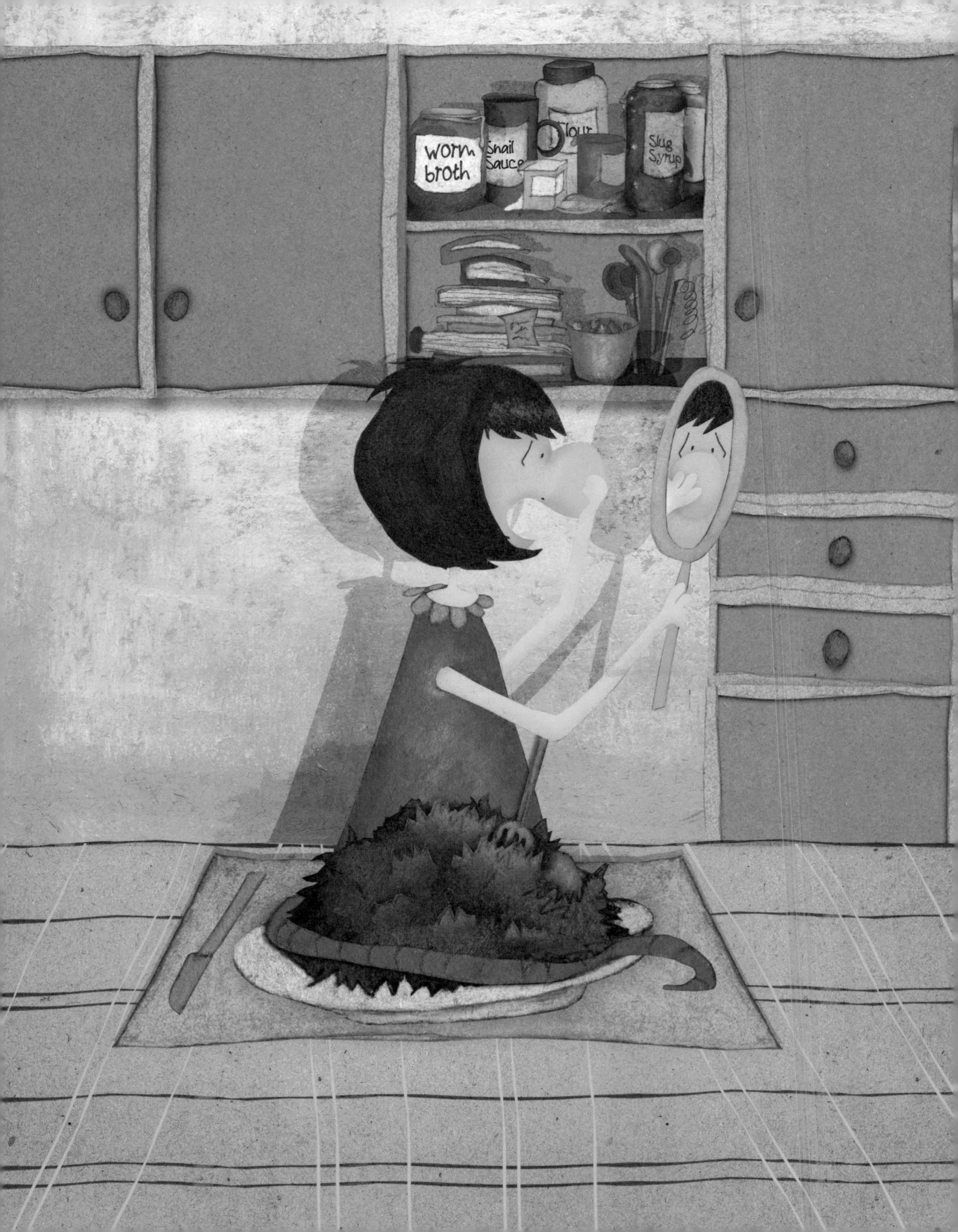
worm broth
Snail Sauce
Flour
Slug Syrup

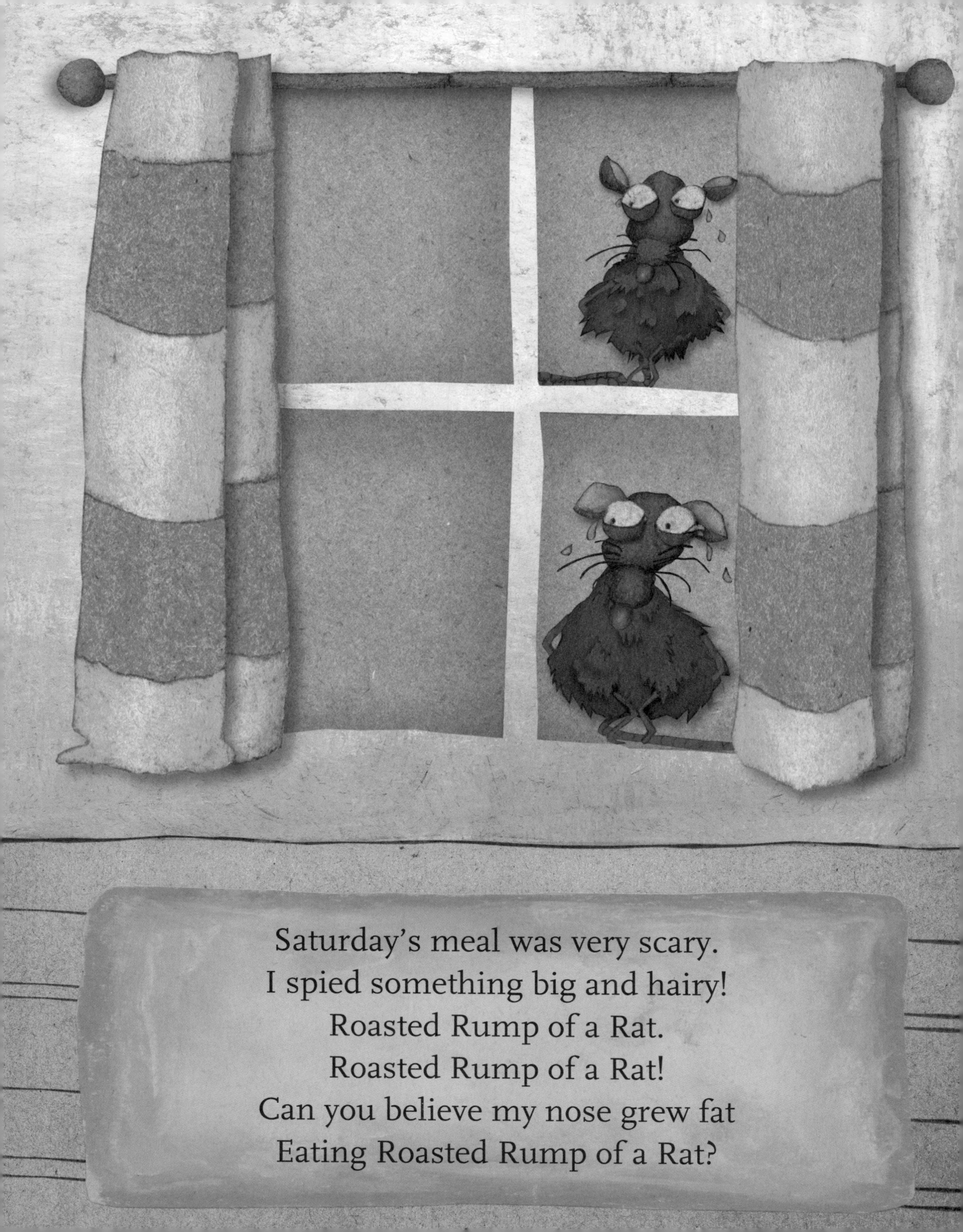

Saturday's meal was very scary.
I spied something big and hairy!
Roasted Rump of a Rat.
Roasted Rump of a Rat!
Can you believe my nose grew fat
Eating Roasted Rump of a Rat?

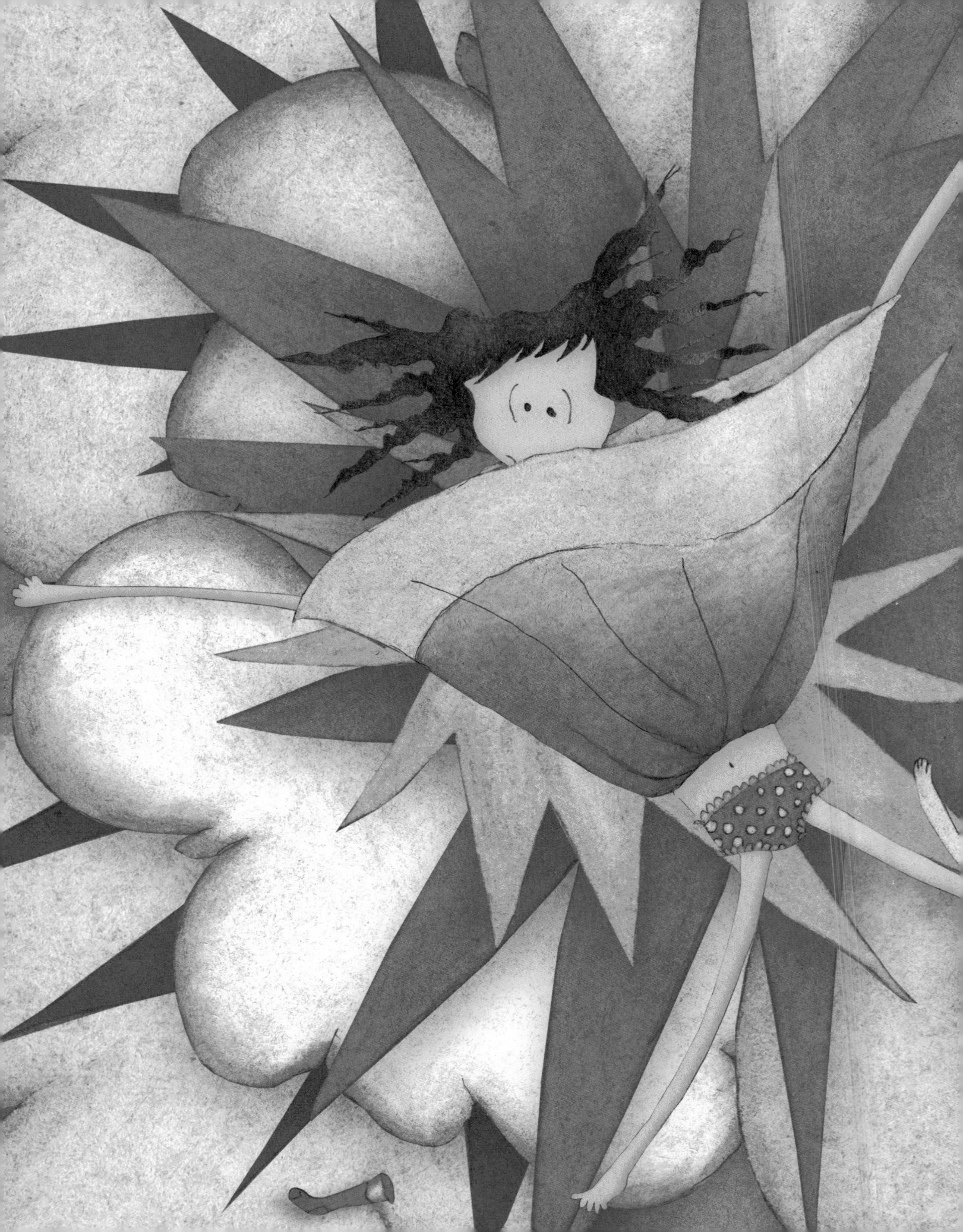

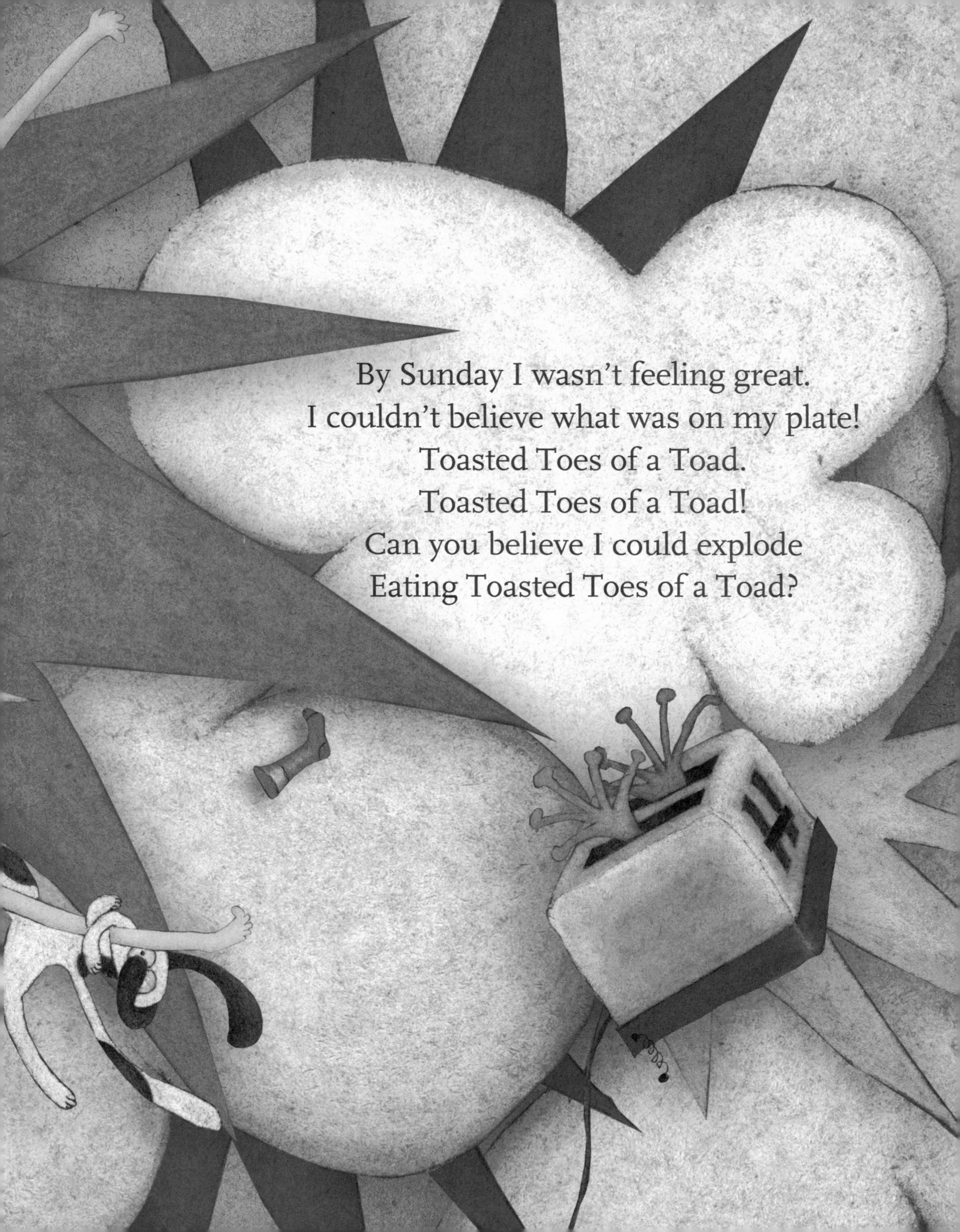

By Sunday I wasn't feeling great.
I couldn't believe what was on my plate!
Toasted Toes of a Toad.
Toasted Toes of a Toad!
Can you believe I could explode
Eating Toasted Toes of a Toad?

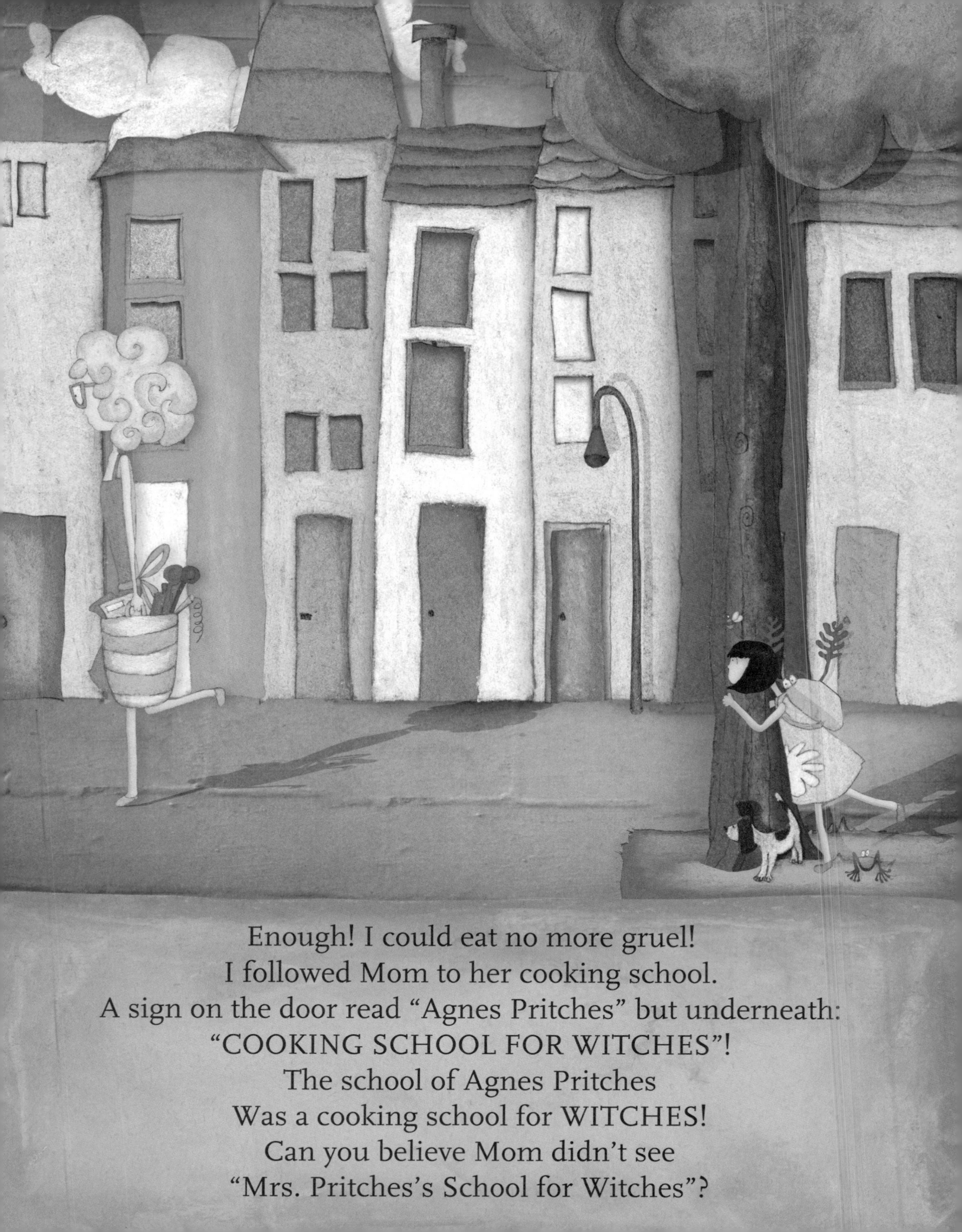

Enough! I could eat no more gruel!
I followed Mom to her cooking school.
A sign on the door read “Agnes Pritches” but underneath:
“COOKING SCHOOL FOR WITCHES”!
The school of Agnes Pritches
Was a cooking school for WITCHES!
Can you believe Mom didn’t see
“Mrs. Pritches’s School for Witches”?

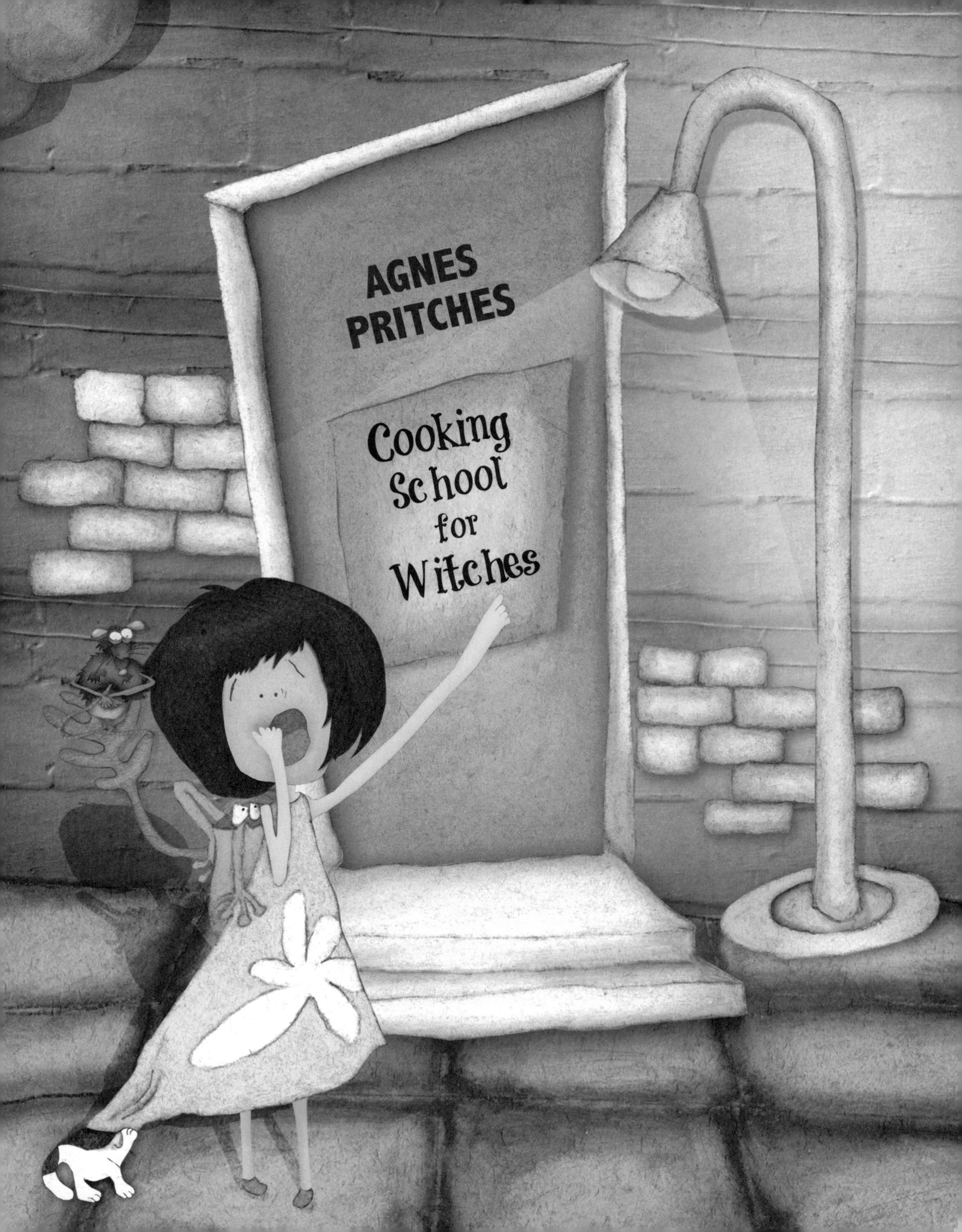
AGNES
PRITCHES
Cooking
School
for
Witches

When I told Mom of her dreadful error,
Her eyes grew big, as if in terror!
"What should I do? Oh, forgive me, please!"
I forgave her and asked for
Macaroni & Cheese!

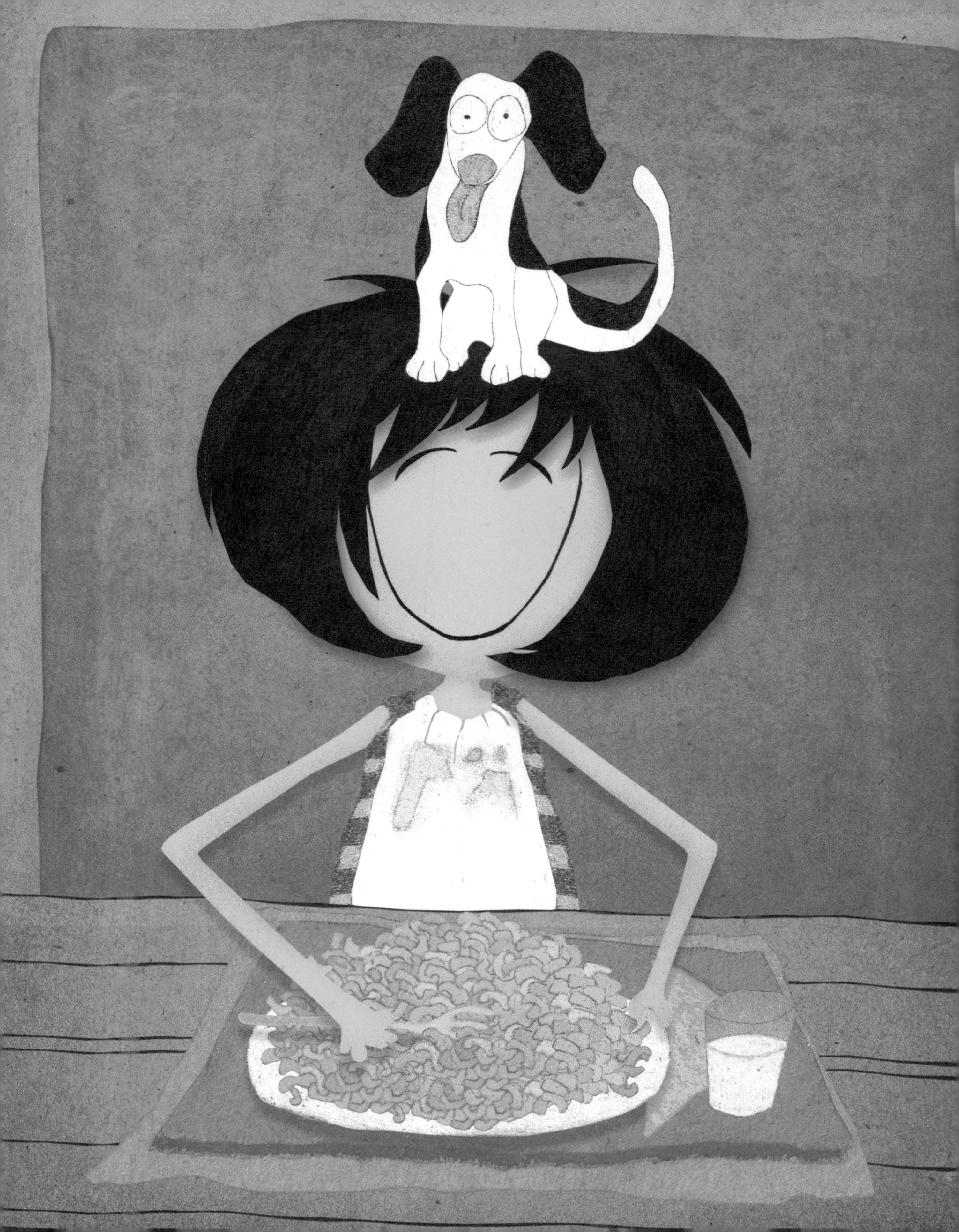

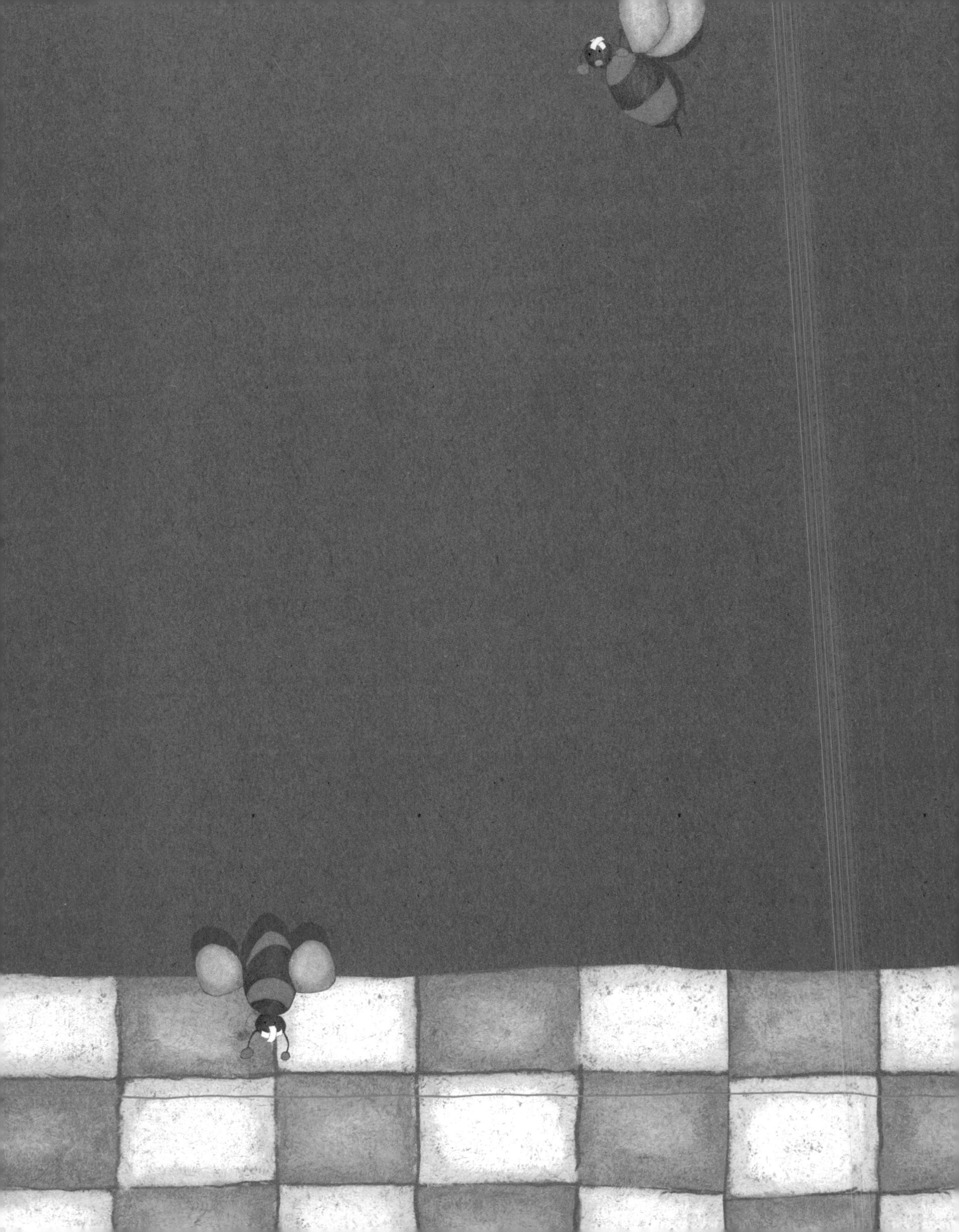

Sky Pony Press books may be purchased in bulk at special discounts for
sales promotion, corporate gifts, fund-raising, or educational purposes.
Special editions can also be created to specifications. For details, contact the
Special Sales Department, Sky Pony Press, 307 West 36th Street, 11th Floor,
New York, NY 10018 or info@skyhorsepublishing.com.

Sky Pony® is a registered trademark of Skyhorse Publishing, Inc.®,
a Delaware corporation.

Visit our website at www.skyponypress.com.

10 9 8 7 6 5 4 3 2 1

Manufactured in China, June 2013
This product conforms to CPSIA 2008

Library of Congress Cataloging-in-Publication Data

Olin, Marilyn.
Mom, mac & cheese, please! / written by Marilyn Orlin ; illustrations by
Dunja Pantic.
pages cm
Summary: After suffering through a series of horrific meals, a young girl
discovers that her mother has been attending a cooking school for witches.
ISBN 978-1-62087-995-5 (hardcover : alk. paper) [1. Stories in rhyme. 2.
Cooking--Fiction. 3. Witches--Fiction.] I. Pantic, Dunja, illustrator. II. Title.
III. Title: Mom, mac and cheese, please!
PZ8.3.O63313Mom 2013
[E]--dc23
2013012201

ISBN: 978-1-62087-995-5

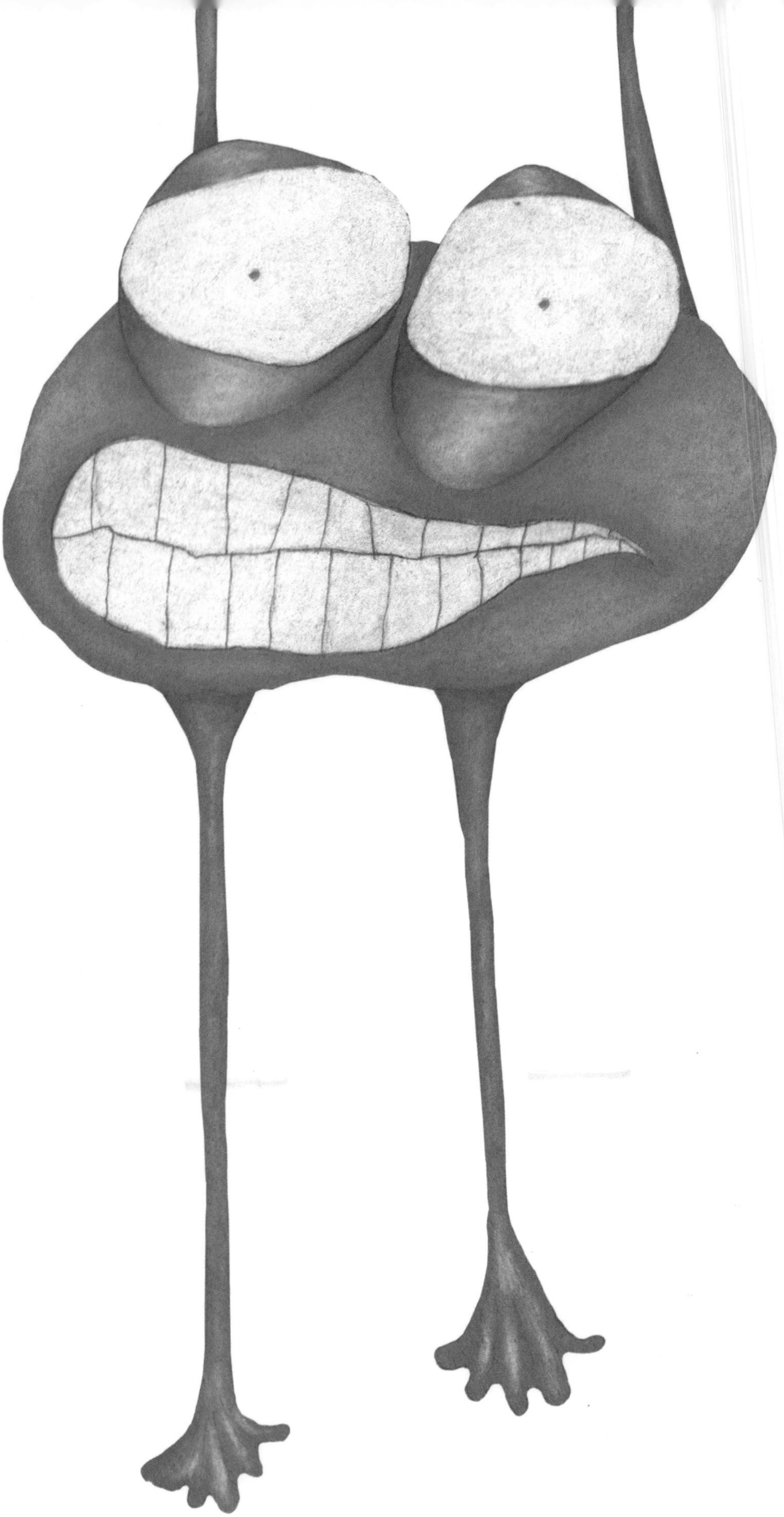